ROTHERHAM LIBRARY & INFORMATION SERVICES

This book must be returned by the date specified at the time of issue
as the DATE DUE FOR RETURN.
The loan may be extended (personally, by post or telephone) for a
further period if the book is not required by another reader, by quoting
the above number / author / title.

LIS7a

For Jess

10 9 8 7 6 5 4

British Library Cataloguing in Publication Data available.

ISBN 0 86264 907 2

This book has been printed on acid-free paper

HOUDINI
the
Disappearing
Hamster

Story by
Terence Blacker

Pictures by
Pippa Unwin

Andersen Press · London

It's time for Houdini the hamster to be given his supper.
But something's wrong.

Houdini's not there.
Oh dear.

The Perfect family next door are having tea.
"Shall I be Mother?" asks Daddy Perfect.

Houdini's here.
But where?

The old lady is getting angry.
The noise from next door is making her teacups rattle.

Houdini's here.
But where?

Today is the twins' birthday.
Their party is getting out of hand.

Houdini's here.
But where?

Mr Wright is playing with his son's train set.
Mrs Wright is calling him a big baby.

Houdini's here.
But where?

David is playing the piano beautifully.
Peter is trying to paint a picture of him.

Houdini's here.
But where?

The dogs have been left all alone.
They want to be out in the park.

Houdini's here.
But where?

The old man had been fast asleep.
He's annoyed that he has been woken up.

Houdini's here.
But where?

The girl down the road has had a terrible fright.
Something small and hairy is in her bathroom.

It's Houdini.
Come here!

Everyone is wondering what the fuss is about.
"Help!" says the girl. "A rat!"

It's not a rat.
It's Houdini.

Mummy is getting worried.
Sometimes she wishes she had never bought that hamster.

There's a ring at the door.
Houdini's here!

More Andersen Press paperback picture books!

OUR PUPPY'S HOLIDAY
by Ruth Brown

NOTHING BUT TROUBLE
by Gus Clarke

FRIGHTENED FRED
by Peta Coplans

THE HILL AND THE ROCK
by David McKee

MR UNDERBED
by Chris Riddell

THE KING BIRD
by A.H. Benjamin and Tony Ross

MICHAEL
by Tony Bradman and Tony Ross

WELL I NEVER!
by Heather Eyles and Tony Ross

FROG IN LOVE
by Max Velthuijs

FROG IS A HERO
by Max Velthuijs

THE LONG BLUE BLAZER
by Jeanne Willis and Susan Varley